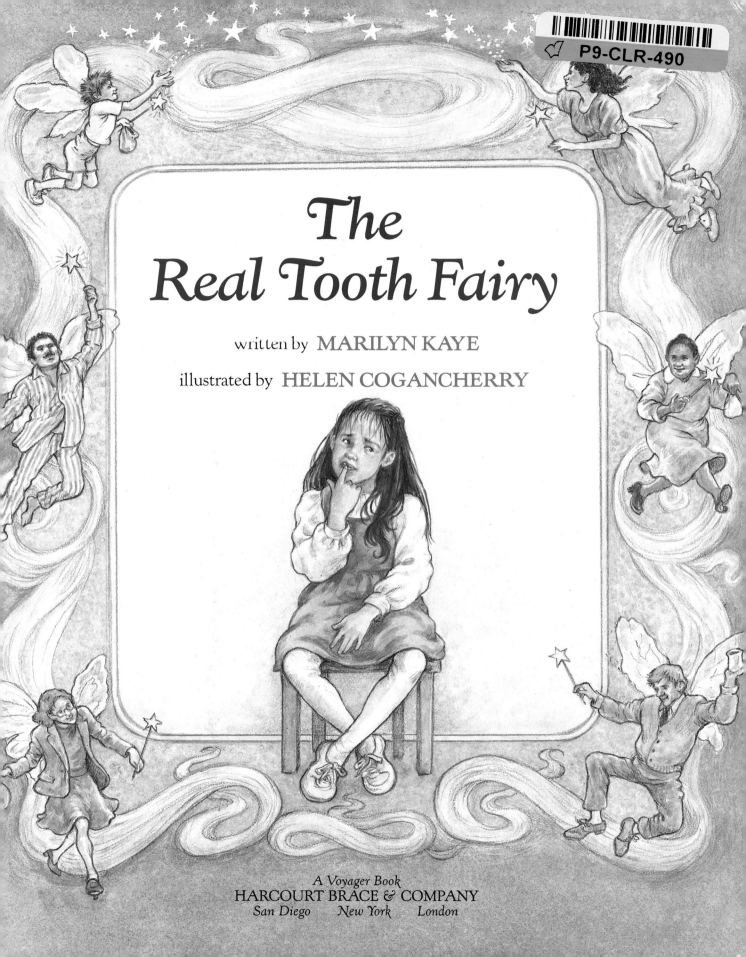

The Real Tooth Fairy

written by MARILYN KAYE

illustrated by HELEN COGANCHERRY

A Voyager Book
HARCOURT BRACE & COMPANY
San Diego   New York   London

Requests for permission to make copies of any part of the work
should be mailed to: Permissions Department,
Harcourt Brace & Company, 6277 Sea Harbor Drive,
Orlando, Florida 32887-6777.

Library of Congress Cataloging-in-Publication Data
Kaye, Marilyn.
The real tooth fairy.
Summary: Elise loses a tooth and discovers the magic of the real tooth fairy.
[1. Tooth fairy—Fiction] I. Cogancherry, Helen, ill.
II. Title.
PZ7.K2127Re 1990   [E]   88-6205
ISBN 0-15-201335-0

Special Edition for Scholastic Book Fairs, Inc.

A B C D E F

Printed in Singapore

The illustrations in this book were done in
watercolor with Negro pencil on Strathmore 2-ply paper.
The display type and the text type were set in ITC Garamond Light.
Composition by Thompson Type, San Diego, California
Color separations were made by Bright Arts, Ltd., Hong Kong.
Printed and bound by Tien Wah Press, Singapore
Production supervision by Warren Wallerstein and Ginger Boyer
Designed by Camilla Filancia

One afternoon at school, Miss Kelly was reading a story, but Elise wasn't listening. Elise was wiggling her tooth. Suddenly, it wasn't there anymore. It was lying on her tongue. Elise reached into her mouth and took it out. She had just lost her first tooth!

Elise wanted to jump out of her seat and tell everyone. She was so excited she could hardly wait until Miss Kelly finished reading.

Finally, Miss Kelly closed her book and said, "It's time to go outside." Elise jumped up and ran to show Ben and Susan.

"Wow! You're lucky," Ben said.

"Don't forget to put it under your pillow for the tooth fairy," Susan reminded Elise.

"What does the tooth fairy look like?" Ben asked Susan.

"I don't know," Susan said. "I've never seen her. Nobody has."

"Well, I'm going to see her," Elise announced. "I'm going to stay awake tonight and wait for her."

"You can't do that," Susan said. "No one is supposed to see the tooth fairy. She won't come if you're not sleeping."

"But I want to see her!" Elise protested.

"Well, you can't," said Susan. "That's the law."

Elise wasn't so sure about that.

That night, Elise carefully placed the tooth under her pillow. Her parents kissed her good night and left the room. But Elise didn't go to sleep. She was thinking. Maybe she could fool the tooth fairy and just pretend to be asleep.

She closed her eyes tightly and curled up in her bed. She was too excited to sleep, so she lay there imagining what the tooth fairy would look like.

She would wear blue, Elise thought, and she would have wings, and there would be a glow all around her. All fairies glowed. Elise was certain of that.

Elise held her breath. Someone was coming! She heard the bedroom door open softly. She lay very still, as if she were frozen, until she felt a hand slide under her pillow. Then, slowly and carefully, she opened her eyes a tiny bit, just a crack.

Elise couldn't believe what she saw. Her mother was standing there. Elise's very own mother was taking her tooth.

Was she dreaming? Could this be true? Elise closed her eyes, silently counted to three, and peeked again. Now her mother was putting something under her pillow. Then she turned away and tip-toed out of the room, closing the door behind her.

Elise felt under her pillow and found a shiny new quarter. She fell back on her bed, thrilled by her amazing discovery: Her mother was the tooth fairy.

Oh, what a lucky girl she was! Some mothers were teachers, or doctors, or fire fighters. Elise's mother was the one and only tooth fairy. Could anything be finer?

The next morning, she checked under her pillow again. The quarter was still there.

She ran downstairs to show her mother and father. "Look what I got!" she said.

"My goodness," her mother exclaimed. "Who gave you that quarter?"

Elise giggled. "Oh, Mommy, you know who gave it to me."

Then her father came in. "Did the tooth fairy visit you last night?"

"Of course she did," Elise said. She looked at her mother, but her mother just smiled.

And then Elise remembered what Susan had told her. Children are supposed to be sleeping when the tooth fairy comes. They're not supposed to see her. That's why her mother hadn't told her she was the tooth fairy.

I'm the only one who knows who the real tooth fairy is, Elise thought. *It's my secret*.

But she couldn't keep the secret to herself for very long. As soon as she got to school, she ran up to Ben. "I'm going to tell you a secret," she said. "Promise you won't tell anyone?"

"Sure," Ben promised.

Elise whispered in his ear. "My mother is the tooth fairy."

Ben was astonished. "How do you know?"

"I stayed awake last night and I saw her," Elise told him.

Ben thought about this. "Maybe you were dreaming."

Elise shook her head. "I was wide awake, honest."

"I don't believe you," Ben said. "Your mother doesn't look like a tooth fairy."

"You don't know what the tooth fairy looks like," Elise told him. "You've never seen her."

"I will tonight." Ben opened his mouth. "My tooth fell out this morning."

After school, Elise told her mother about Ben's tooth. "Mommy, do you know that Ben lives on Oak Street?"

Her mother wasn't listening. She was busy opening a bag of cookies.

Elise frowned. Would her mother go to the right house? She tried not to worry about it. After all, the tooth fairy must know where all children live. That was her job.

That night, Elise dreamed of her mother, the tooth fairy. She was entering Ben's bedroom, softly and gently sliding a hand under his pillow. Then Ben opened his eyes, just a little bit, and saw her there. His eyes got wider and wider. Elise was telling the truth! Her mother was the tooth fairy!

Then her mother left, adding Ben's tooth to her bag full of baby teeth. And what did she do with them all? Why, she went outside, gathered the teeth in her hands, and thrust them above her. They rose higher and higher, until they hung suspended, shining in the night sky. They had turned into stars!

It was all so real, Elise wasn't quite sure if she was really dreaming. She couldn't wait to get to school the next morning and find out what Ben had seen. She ran up to him in class.

"Did the tooth fairy come? Did you see her?"

Ben nodded. "I stayed awake and waited. But guess what? You were wrong. Your mother isn't the tooth fairy. My father is!"

Elise was shocked. "That's not true," she accused Ben.

"I saw her. I saw the tooth fairy. And it was my mother."

"Well, I saw the tooth fairy, too," Ben replied. "And it was my father."

"You must have been dreaming," Elise argued.

Ben shook his head. "Nope, I was wide awake."

Elise got angry. "You're making that up!"

"No I'm not!" Ben shouted.

They glared at each other.

"Let's ask Susan," Elise suggested. Ben followed her to Susan's seat.

"I saw the tooth fairy," Elise told Susan. "And it was my mother."

"I saw the tooth fairy, too," Ben said. "It was my father."

"Who do you believe?" Elise demanded.

Susan thought about this. "You were both dreaming," she said firmly.

Elise didn't think so. But it was all very confusing. Who was the real tooth fairy? She had to know the truth.

When she got home, she went directly to her mother. "Mommy, are you the tooth fairy?" she asked.

Her mother looked at her in surprise. "Why do you think I'm the tooth fairy?"

"Because I saw you come into my room and take my tooth," Elise told her. "But Ben says his father is the tooth fairy. Who's right? Me or Ben?"

Her mother was quiet for a moment. Then she sat down, and pulled Elise close to her.

"Let me tell you a story," she said. "Once upon a time, the tooth fairy went to a little boy's room to get his tooth. While she was there, the little boy woke up. He didn't know about the tooth fairy, and he was frightened when he saw a stranger in his room. He started to cry."

"What did the tooth fairy do?" Elise asked.

"Well, she was very sorry that she made the little boy cry. And she didn't want that to happen to any boy or girl, ever again."

"So the tooth fairy decided from that day on, whenever she visited a child's room, she wouldn't be a stranger. She would make herself look like someone the child knows and recognizes."

"How can she do that?" Elise wanted to know.

"The tooth fairy has magic," her mother answered. "She can look like anyone she wants to look like. And that's why the tooth fairy might look like your mother for you, or Ben's father for Ben. And for every little boy or girl, she looks like someone that child loves and trusts."

Slowly Elise nodded. It was beginning to make sense.

"I think I have another loose tooth," she said. She opened her mouth and showed her mother.

"You're right," her mother said. "And when it falls out, the tooth fairy will come again."

"And she'll look like you," Elise said.

"Maybe," her mother replied. "Or she might look like Daddy. Remember, the tooth fairy can look like anyone you love."

Elise felt good. Now she knew the truth about the tooth fairy. And the next day, she told her mother's story to Ben and Susan.

"So that's why you saw your mother and I saw my father," Ben said.

"Of course, the next time she might not look like your father," Elise reminded him. "Remember, she can look like anyone you love."

"Gee," Ben said. "That means the next time I lose a tooth, the tooth fairy might look like my mother. Or my big brother."

"Or maybe it will be Miss Kelly," Susan said. "If I woke up at night

and saw Miss Kelly, I wouldn't be scared."

"The tooth fairy can look like anyone you love," Elise said. "I love lots of people. Maybe next time she'll look like my doctor, or my grandmother, or the lady in the pet shop."

"Or my Aunt Elinor," Susan said.

"Or my babysitter," offered Ben.

Elise sighed. "I *still* wish I could see what she really looks like." She touched her tooth. It was getting looser.

Every day, she wiggled her tooth, and every day it moved more and more. Finally, one bright day, it fell out.

That night, Elise placed her tooth under the pillow, and she lay down. She wanted to stay awake, but she was very, very sleepy. She tried to keep her eyes open, but they kept closing. *Wake up, wake up*, she told herself.

And then she heard someone come into her room. She opened her eyes and looked at the tooth fairy. The fairy had her mother's face, and her mother's hair, and her mother's nightgown. In fact, she looked exactly like her mother. But Elise knew better.

This time she didn't even bother to pretend she was sleeping. She sat up straight.

"Oh, tooth fairy, please let me see you as you really are. I promise I won't cry."

The tooth fairy smiled. And suddenly, there was light all around her. The nightgown grew longer, and wider, and soon it was a real gown, soft and blue and sparkling, like a night sky full of stars. On her head, a glittering crown appeared. In her hand, there was a wand, with a shining star at the tip. And she had wings, glorious wings, so light and delicate Elise could see right through them.

She was the most beautiful person Elise had ever seen, and she looked just like a tooth fairy should look.

But only for a moment. Then the wings began to fade, and soon they disappeared. The wand and the crown vanished. The sparkling gown seemed to melt away, until it was only a plain nightgown. And now the tooth fairy looked like her mother again, not sparkling, not glittering, but just as beautiful.

Elise had seen the real tooth fairy. And now she could dream about her all night long.